Leo Lionni

Pezzettino

Pantheon

Copyright © 1975 by Leo Lionni. All rights reserved under International and Pan-American Copyright Conventions.
Published in the United States by Pantheon Books, a division of Random House, Inc., New York, and simultaneously in
Canada by Random House of Canada Limited, Toronto. LIBRARY OF CONGRESS CATALOGING IN PUBLICATION DATA. Lionni,
Leo, 1910-   . Pezzettino. SUMMARY: Little Pezzettino is so small he is convinced he must be a piece of somebody else. A
wise man helps him discover the truth. [1. Identity—Fiction]   I. Title.   PZ7.L6634Pe [E] 75-9669   ISBN 0-394-83156-X
ISBN 0-394-93156-4 lib. bdg.   First Edition 0 9 8 7 6 5 4 3 2   Manufactured in the United States of America

Pezzettino

His name was Pezzettino.* All the others were big and did daring and wonderful things. He was small and surely must be a little piece of somebody else, he thought. He often wondered whose little piece he could be, and one day he decided to find out.

_____

*_Pezzettino, in Italian, means "little piece."_
It is pronounced "pet-set-eeno"

"Excuse me," he asked the one-who-runs, "am I perhaps your little piece?"

"How could I possibly run if I had a piece missing?" said the one-who-runs, somewhat surprised.

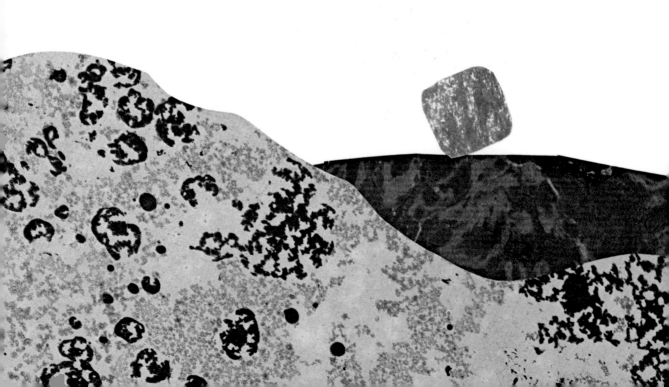

"Am I your little piece?" he asked the strong-one.
"How could I be strong if I had a piece missing?"
was the answer.

And when the swimming-one came up to the surface,
Pezzettino asked him too.

"How could I swim if I had a piece missing?" answered
the swimming-one. And he dove back into the deep water.

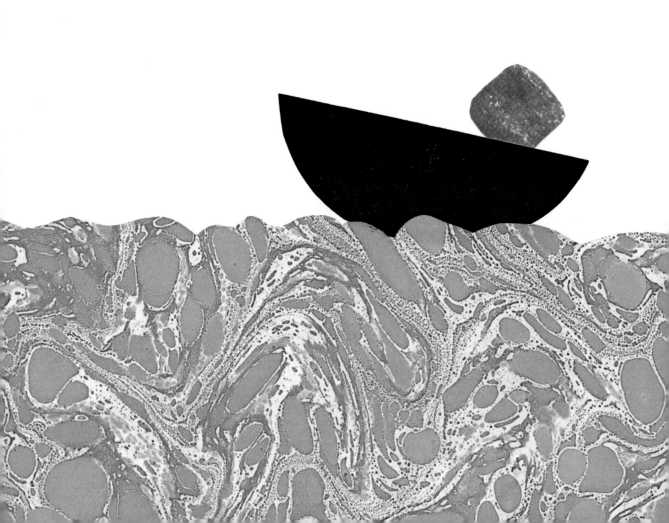

"You up there!" shouted Pezzettino as he climbed toward the one-on-the-mountain. "Am I a little piece of yours?"

The one-on-the-mountain laughed. "Do you think I could climb mountains if I had a piece missing?"

Pezzettino asked the flying-one too. But the answer was always the same.

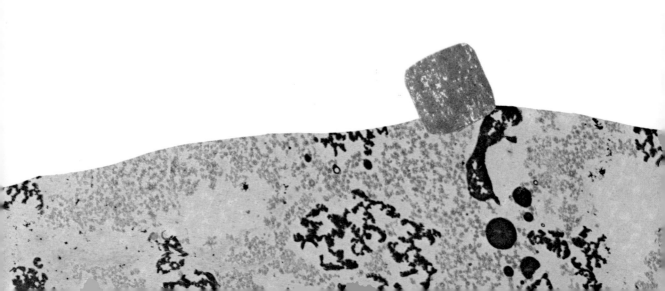

Finally Pezzettino went to the wise-one who lived in a cave. "Wise-one," he said, "am I a little piece of yours?"

"Do you think I could be wise if I had a little piece missing?" answered the wise-one.

"I must be *someone's* little piece?" Pezzettino cried out. "How can I find out?"

"Go to the Island of Wham," said the wise-one.

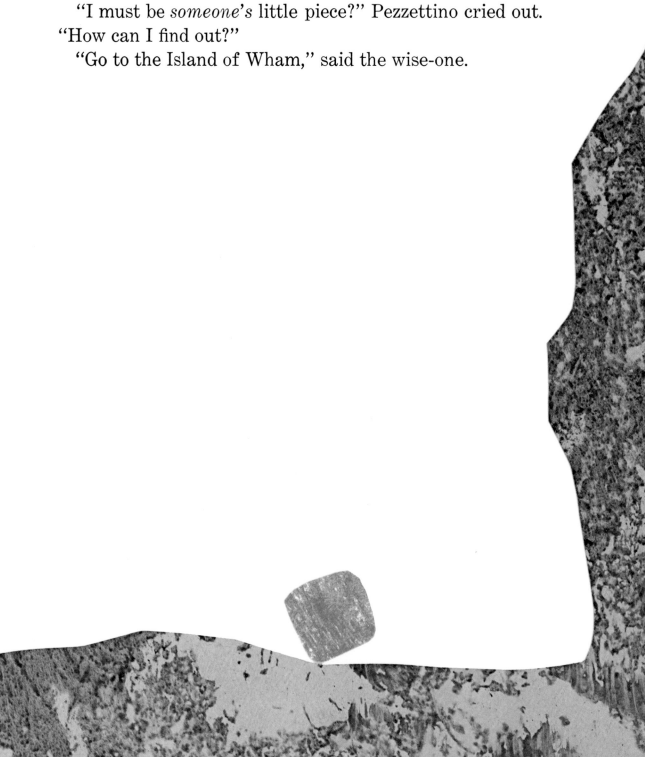

Early the next morning Pezzettino took off in his little boat.

After a rough trip on the high sea, he arrived wet and tired on the Island of Wham.

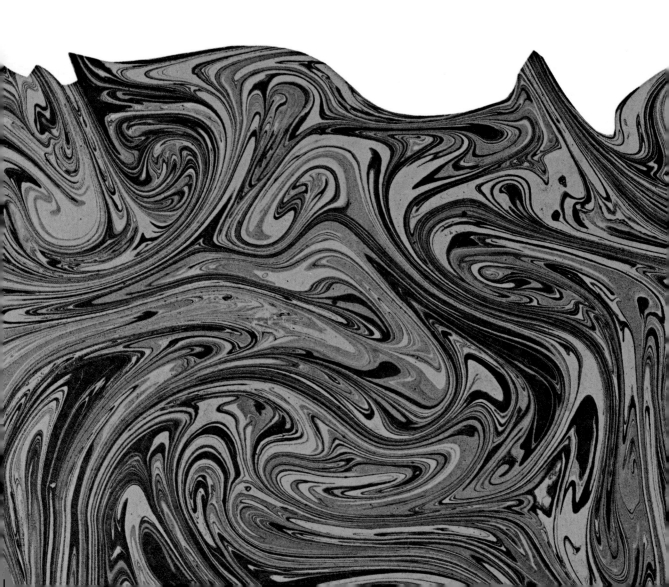

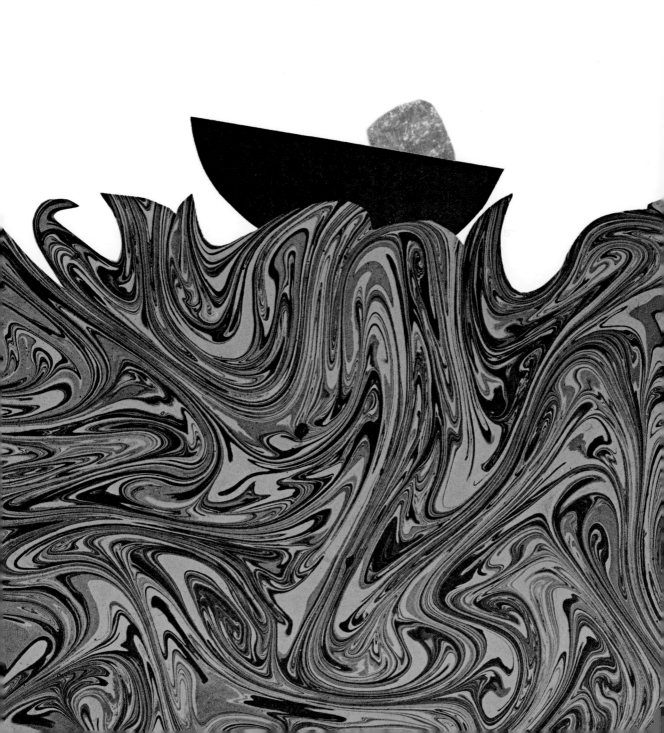

How strange! The island was nothing but heaps of pebbles. Not a tree, not a blade of grass. And above all, not a single living creature.

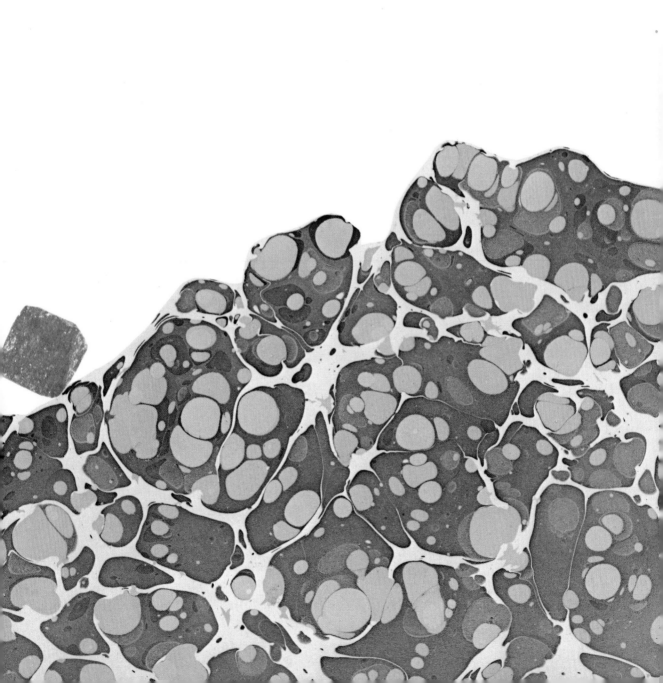

Pezzettino climbed up and down, up and down, until finally, exhausted, he tripped, tumbled down . . .

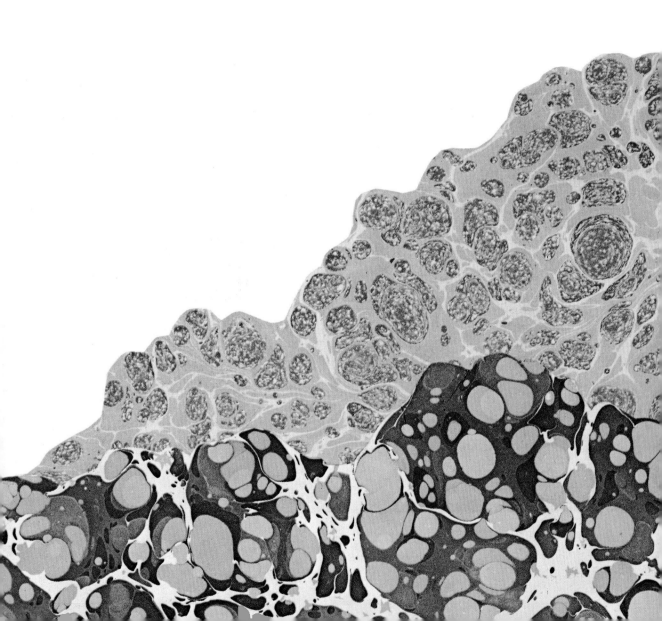

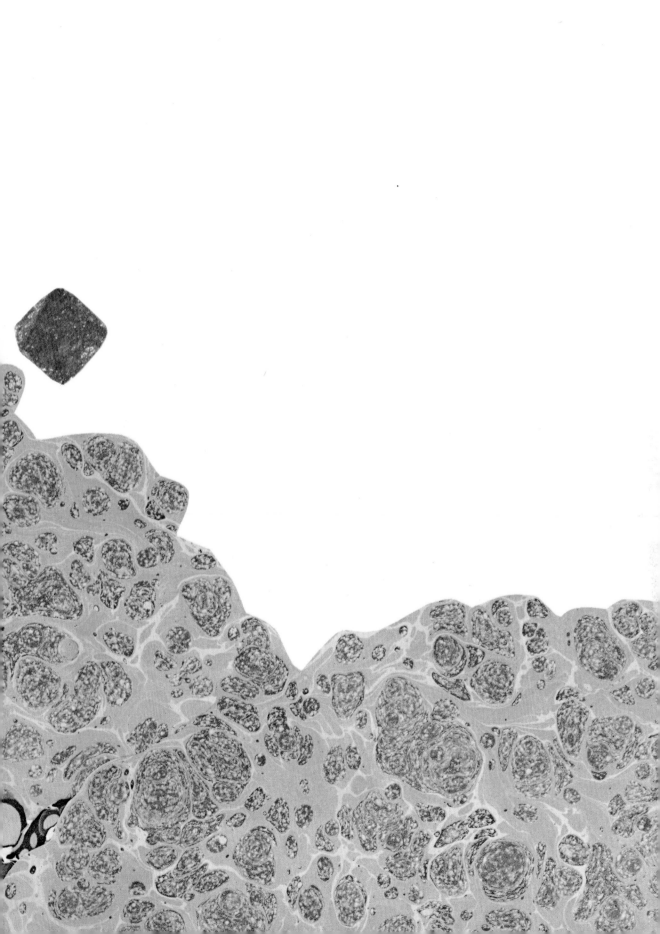

. . . and broke into lots of little pieces!
The wise-one had been right. Pezzettino now knew that he too, like all the others, was made of little pieces.

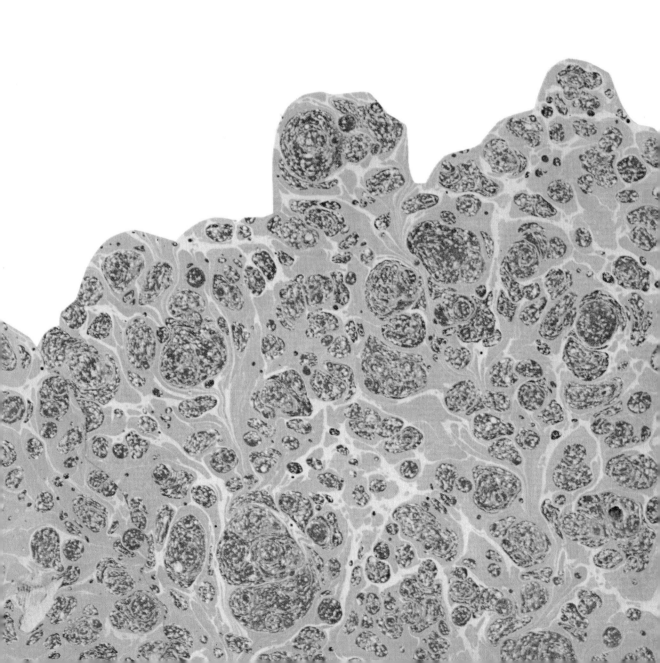

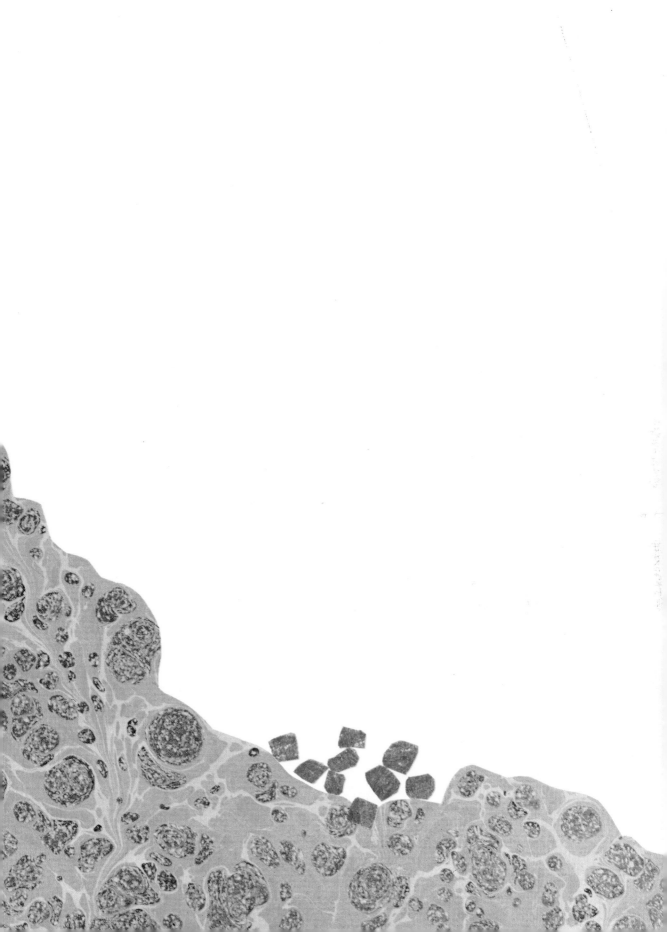

He picked himself up, and when he was sure there was not a single little piece missing, he ran back to his boat.

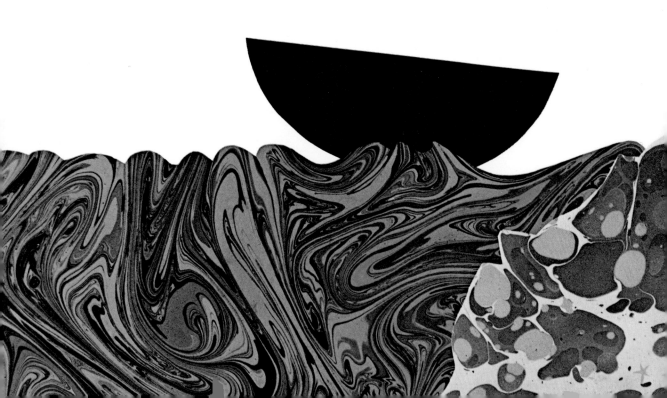

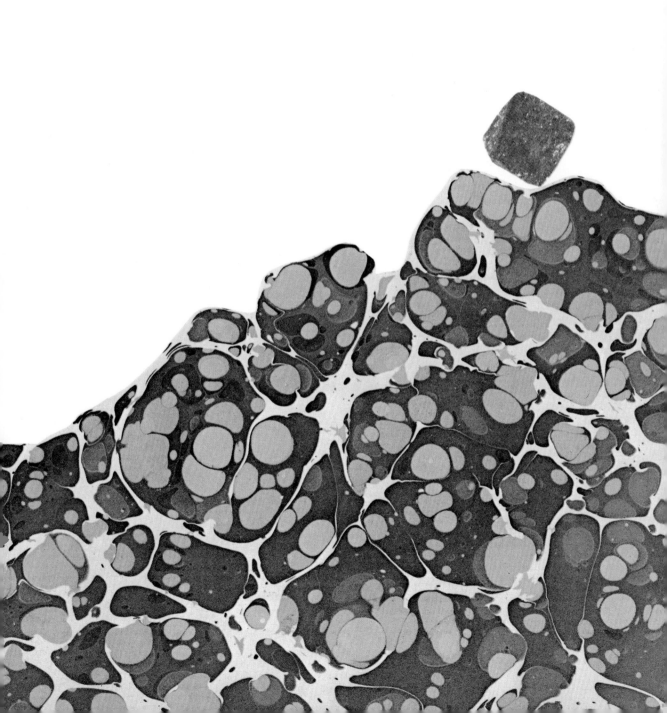

He rowed all night to get home as fast as he could.

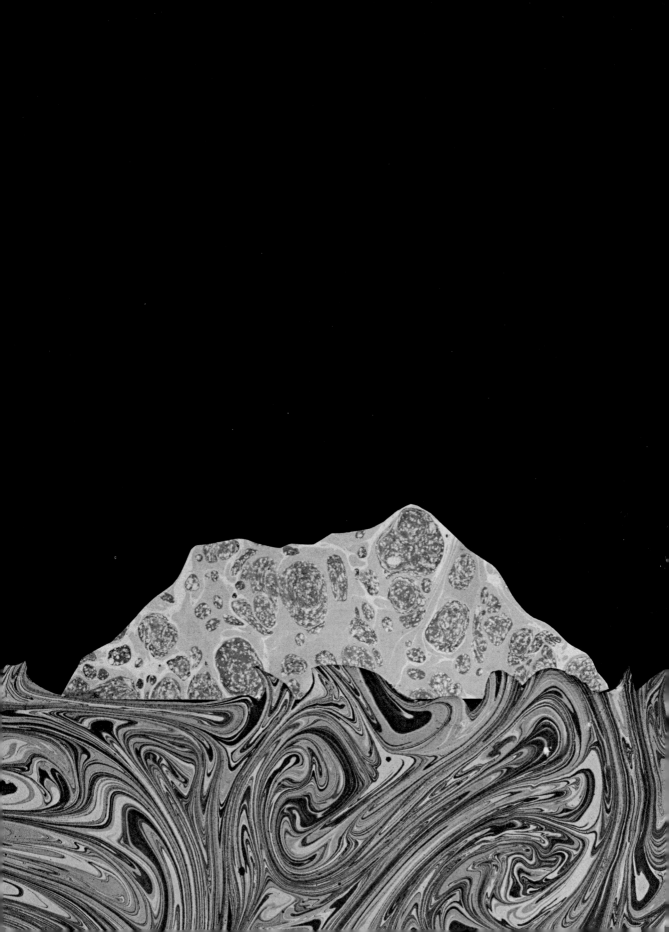

All his friends were waiting for him.
"I am myself!" he shouted full of joy.
His friends didn't quite understand what he meant,
but Pezzettino seemed happy, and so they were happy too.